SO GOOD YOU CAN'T STOP READING THEM!

Where Is That Dog?

Written by Marilyn Pitt & Jane Hileman

Illustrated by John Bianchi

Dog!
Where are you?

3

Here, dog!
Come here!

Come, dog.
Where are you?

You come here!
Come, dog. Come!

9

Are you in here?
Where are you?

There you are!